Printed in the United States of America

First Printing, 2016
ISBN 9 -780997-9249-0-9
R.J. Henry Publishing
6929 N. Hayden Road, Suite C4-283
Scottsdale, Arizona 85250-7970

BUDDY
THE SOLDIER BEAR

Written by Marie Joy
Illustrated by Brandon Pollard

Acknowledgements

Thank you to my husband Scott for always being in my corner no matter what, never trying to tame my creative--sometimes wild--spirit. You put up with me even though I know that I drove you crazy at times through the madness of writing and launching this book. Thanks for your help with editing, for always believing in me, and accepting that this project would become a reality, without ever questioning it.

Thank you to my sons Ryan and Jeremy for always encouraging me to keep plugging along with the book, even through the obstacles. Thanks for always believing in me and letting me run my ideas by you. You both make me want to be a better person. You're both amazing young men, and I'm proud to be your mom.

Thank you to my illustrator Brandon, who brought Buddy to life. You are incredibly talented, and I truly never could have done it without you. You really are my third son.

Thank you to Rachel for your help with the website. You have mad skills and I really appreciate your help.

Thank you to Ann Videan, my book shepherd/guru, for your help and patience with editing, layout and marketing. You helped make my dream become a reality.

Thank you to all of my family, friends and coworkers who said, "You can do this!" rather than, "Are you crazy?" when I said I was writing a book. Though there are too many of you to mention each by name, your support did not go unnoticed. Your encouragement helped me believe that this could become a reality.

Thank you to all the wonderful women at the Scottsdale Society of Women Writers for warmly welcoming me into your group, for sharing what you have learned on your own writing journeys, and for helping me to believe that I could actually be a writer.

Thank you to everyone who has selflessly served in our military, especially during times of war, with a special appreciation to the "Greatest Generation" who bravely fought in World War II.

Dedication

For my amazing grandsons Jackson, Cooper, and Bennett, who taught me to believe in magic again. You can be anything that you want to be, my little loves. May the three of you dream big, and may all of your dreams come true!

For my dad Henry, who fought in WW II, served in the United States Army and Air Force for twenty years, and was always an example of kindness and service to others. I only wish that he had lived long enough to see this dream become a reality.

For my oldest son Ryan, who served in the United States Army in Iraq and Afghanistan and proudly carried on my father's legacy.

For every soldier who wrote back to me when I sent them a care package and has kept in touch with me over the years. You became the inspiration for this book and I truly consider you my adopted sons and daughters.

Buddy was a very lonely bear.

His whole life
he had been all alone
on a high shelf
in a toy store.

He didn't wear a fancy outfit or
sing songs when you squeezed him.

He **longed** to be a part of a
loving family.
He **dreamed** of doing **amazing things**
and traveling to **faraway lands**.

One day, a nice lady pulled him down from the high shelf.

She hugged him and said, "You'll do just fine."

She taped him up inside a big box.

Buddy's heart pounded.
He wondered, "Where am I going?"

Lots of **strange noises**
came from outside of his box.

Time **dragged** on.
It **felt** like he was in there **forever!**

The box finally stopped
moving.

Light spilled in, as the lid began to open.

Suddenly a **young man** with a strange **uniform** pulled him into the **air** and said, "*Hey, Buddy!*"

The man and his friends passed **Buddy** around and **played** with him. They took him on **many adventures.**

Buddy flew in **helicopters.**

He **jumped** out of **airplanes.**

Buddy and the soldiers took **long rides** in the **country.**

Sometimes Buddy grew **nervous** on their **adventures.**

Buddy knew that the **soldiers** would **protect** him, because he was part of their family.

One day, a favorite soldier
packed up Buddy with all of his
gear...

...and took him on a
long plane ride.

It wasn't one of their more
exciting adventures,
but the **soldiers** seemed so **happy!**

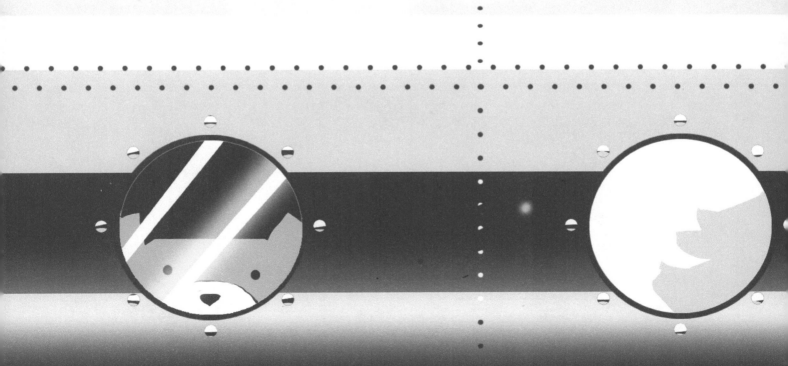

When they landed, a **little boy** ran to the soldier...

...and gave **Buddy** the **tightest hug** he ever felt.

The little boy grinned up at his dad.
"You're home!"
Buddy had experienced some
awesome adventures!

He had done **amazing things** and traveled to **faraway lands!** Joy grew in Buddy's heart, knowing he had become part of a **loving military family** and all of his **dreams** had come true!

About the author:

The military has always held a special place in Marie's heart. Her dad served in WWII and her oldest son served in Iraq and Afghanistan. She founded and ran a nonprofit organization called Operation Hugs From Home when her son was first deployed. The organization sent thousands of care packages to deployed military service men and women. She now is a part of her local chapter of the Blue Star Mothers of America. They serve our military in a number of ways, including sending care packages. Marie also joined her local American Legion Auxiliary, to serve the military in more ways.

While sending care packages, Marie often dreamed of writing a children's story that could give back to our brave warriors. With Buddy's story, Marie hopes to inspire children to dream big and to bring awareness to military and veteran causes.

To help fulfill her dream of creating something to give back to soldiers in a big way, a portion of the proceeds from this book will go to nonprofit organizations who help soldiers and veterans.

Marie Joy grew up in Massachusetts and New Jersey. She currently resides with her husband in Scottsdale, Arizona. She loves to travel and is a self-proclaimed "cruise addict," though one of her favorite destinations is Kentucky where she visits her beloved grandsons.

About The illustrator:

Brandon J. Pollard grew up in the military life with his dad, who served twenty years in the Air Force. He lived and visited many places growing up, like England and the Philippines. After high school, he joined the Army. He served nine years with the active Army and National Guard as a CH47D Helicopter Flight Engineer. He served in Iraq, Afghanistan, and deployed natural-disaster relief efforts following Hurricane Katrina and in Kashmir, Pakistan, after the Earthquake in 2005.

When he left the Army, Brandon relocated to Portland, Oregon, to live closer to his son and family. He attended the Portland Art Institute and graduated with honors in 2015, earning a bachelors degree in Media Arts and Animation.

Brandon now works freelance as an illustrator and graphic designer. Most days, he likes to daydream about old friends, strange places, fast motorcycles, and Jiu Jitsu—and uses them as inspiration for his creative endeavors.

CPSIA information can be obtained
at www.ICGtesting.com
Printed in the USA
LVHW070311130320
649945LV00010B/509